# Noise! Noise! Noise!

By Carl Sommer
Illustrated by Kennon James

*Advance* PUBLISHING INC • HOUSTON

Permissions
Advance Publishing, Inc.
6950 Fulton St.
Houston, TX 77022

www.advancepublishing.com

First Edition
Printed in Singapore

**Library of Congress Cataloging-in-Publication Data**

Sommer, Carl, 1930-
  Noise! noise! noise! / Carl Sommer ; illustrated by Kennon James.--1st ed.
    p. cm. -- (Another Sommer-Time Story)
  "Fun times with tolerance, caring, appreciation"--T.p.
  Summary: Two mice are unhappy with living in the forest, until they move to a farmhouse and discover how good things had been before.
  ISBN 1-57537-020-4 (hardcover: alk. paper). -- ISBN 1-57537-069-7 (library binding: alk. paper)
  [1. Mice--Fiction. 2. Animals--Fiction. 3. Contentment Fiction.] I. James, Kennon, ill. II Title. III. Series: Sommer, Carl, 1930- Another Sommer-Time Story.
PZ7.S696235 Nm 2003
[E]--dc21

                                                              2002026261

# Noise! Noise! Noise!

Even though Marcus and Marcella had a beautiful home in the forest, they were always miserable. But all the other animals were very happy living in the forest.

"Work! Work! Work!" complained Marcus.
"I hate that every day we have to work so hard
to find our food."

"Me, too," groaned Marcella. "I'd be so happy to live where it would be easy to find our food."

One day some crows flew to the big tree by Marcus and Marcella's house. They began to sing, "Caw! Caw! Caw!"

"The crows are making too much noise,"

complained Marcella. "It's giving me a headache. Tell the crows to quit making so much noise."

"Quit yelling!" shouted Marcus. "You're making too much noise."

One of the crows flew down from the tree and explained, "We're not yelling, we're singing."

"We don't like to hear your singing," said Marcus. "You make too much noise. Why don't you go to the farm and sing?"

"We like to sing in this big tree," explained the crow. "Why don't *you* go to the farm if you don't like our singing?"

Then the happy crows began to sing, "Caw! Caw! Caw!"

"Noise! Noise! Noise!" complained Marcella. "Ohhhhh! How I wish we could find a place to live that has lots of food and no noise."

"Me, too," groaned Marcus. "But I don't know where we can find such a place."

Then two beavers began chopping down a tree.
"Chop! Chop! Chop!" went the busy beavers.

"The beavers are making too much noise," complained Marcella. "Tell the beavers to quit chopping down the tree and making so much noise."

"Quit chopping down the tree!" yelled Marcus. "You're making too much noise!"

Papa Beaver walked over and said, "We need to cut down trees to build a house for our family."

Papa Beaver immediately went back to work.
"Chop! Chop! Chop!" went the busy beavers.
"Noise! Noise! Noise!" complained Marcella.
"I wish we could find a place to live without so
much noise."

"It surely would be good to find a quiet place to live," said Marcus.

"Ohhhhh!" sighed Marcella. "That would be so wonderful! Then I'd be the happiest mouse in the whole world!"

Then some chipmunks came to play tag by their favorite log.

"Chip! Chip! Chip!" yelled the happy chip-munks as they ran and jumped all over the log.

"The chipmunks are making too much noise," complained Marcella. "Tell them to stop making so much noise."

"Quit yelling!" screamed Marcus. "You're making too much noise!"

"We're not yelling," said the happy chipmunks. "We're playing tag."

"My head! My head!" groaned Marcella. "All this noise is giving me a headache."

"I hate this noise, too," said Marcus. "If only we could find a quiet place to live that has lots of food."

"Ohhhh!!!!" said Marcella. "That would be so, so wonderful!"

One of the chipmunks heard them speaking. He came over and said, "At the farmhouse they have lots of good food and no noise."

"They do?" asked a surprised Marcella.

"Yes, they do," said the chipmunk.

"Thank you!" said Marcus. "We're moving right away from this noisy place."

"Oh good!" said Marcella, beaming from ear to

ear. "I'm so glad we finally found a place to live where we can eat all the food we want without having to search for it every day."

"And no noise!" added Marcus.

"Ohhhhh!" said Marcella. "That would be so, so wonderful! I *know* I will be the happiest mouse in the *whole* world! Let's leave right away!"

Marcus called the beavers and the crows to tell them what was happening. "We've got good news! We're so excited that we have found a

place to live where there's lots of good food to eat and no noise. We're moving there today! Now you can make all the noise you want."

"Why are you moving?" asked Papa Beaver. "Here in the forest you have a nice home and always enough food to eat. You need to appreciate what you have."

"We hate searching for food every day," complained Marcus. "It's too much work."

Marcella put her hands to her ears and said, "And all the noise in the forest gives me a headache. We're moving today!"

"Living on the farm can be very dangerous," warned Mama Beaver. "If the farmer..."

"Thank you for your advice," said Marcella. She did not want to hear what Mama Beaver had to say. Then Marcella said, "We *know* that if the farm has no noise and lots of food we'll be the happiest mice in the whole world!"

"That's right," said Marcus. "We're moving *today*!"

As they began packing, Marcella said, "Since
we're going to such a nice house to live, we don't
have to take so much with us."

"That's right," said Marcus. "We'll just pack a
few things. I'm so glad we don't have to live any

longer in this noisy place."

"I'm so happy, too" said Marcella, beaming from ear to ear. "I can't wait until we get there. Let's hurry up and pack."

"Okay," said Marcus.

As they were walking to their new home, Marcella said, "I'm so happy. Soon we'll have lots of good food to eat and no noise."

"And no more searching for food," said Marcus.

"That's right!" said Marcella. "This is going to be so wonderful!"

When they came over the hill, Marcella's eyes lit up. "Look!" she said. "I see the farm!"

"Oh good!" exclaimed Marcus. Then he suddenly stopped. "Shhhhh!" he whispered. "I think I hear someone talking."

Marcella turned around and saw the farmer and his wife. "Run as fast as you can to the shed," she said softly. "We mustn't let them see us."

They made a quick dash for the shed.

They slid under the shed door and hid. "Whew!" said Marcella, shaking all over. "That sure was sca-a-a-r-r-r-y."

"It-it-it su-su-sure was," stuttered Marcus.

They waited until the farmer and his wife left.

"How can we get into the house?" wondered Marcella. "The door is locked."

Marcus peeked out from under the shed door and said, "I see an open window."

"Let's run to the house and jump onto the windowsill," said Marcella.

"Great idea!" said Marcus.

Marcella ran and jumped onto the windowsill. Marcus followed.

Marcus and Marcella jumped off the windowsill and onto the table. "Wow!!!" shouted Marcus. "Look at all this food!"

"What are we waiting for," said Marcella. Immediately they began munching on the delicious food.

Marcus and Marcella ate and ate and ate. They filled their tummies until they could hold no more.

"Mmmmm!!! Mmmmm!!! Mmmmm!!!!" said Marcus rubbing his tummy. "I never ate such

delicious food in all my life! Now we can eat all
we want without even searching for it."

"And no noise," said Marcella. "This is so,
so wonderful! It can't get any better. I'm the
*happiest* mouse in the *whole* world!"

Just then the door opened—the farmer and his wife walked into the house. "Quick!" screamed Marcella. "Run as fast as you can and hide!"

They jumped off the table and ran. "Look!" yelled the farmer's wife. "A mouse! Quick! Get a broom!"

The farmer grabbed a broom and chased Marcus.

"Hurryyyyy!!!!!" screamed the farmer's wife. "Get that mouse!"

Marcus ran and hid under a rag.

"We must catch that mouse," said the farmer's wife. "I will *not* have a mouse in *my* house!"

While the farmer and his wife were searching for Marcus, Marcella quickly hopped onto the windowsill and jumped out. Marcella dashed to the shed.

The farmer kept searching for Marcus. When he picked up the rag, Marcus jumped up and ran. "Get him!" screamed the farmer's wife. "Get him!"

The farmer chased Marcus into a corner of the room. Whammmm!!!! went the broom.

The broom just missed Marcus. He dashed to the window and jumped out. Then he ran as fast as he could to the shed.

"Let's go back to the forest to live," said Marcella, trembling. "I think it will be just fine living with noise and searching for food every day."

"I-I-I think so, too!" stuttered Marcus. "L-L-Let's leave *right now*!"

As they were walking back to the forest, Marcella said, "Living in the farmhouse was terrible.  I'm so glad we're going back to our home in the forest."

"Me, too," said Marcus.

When Marcus and Marcella came back, the forest animals came to visit them. "Did the farm have lots of food?" asked a crow.

"The farm had lots of good food," said Marcus.

"Did the farm have lots of noise?" asked Papa Beaver.

"No," said Marcella. "It was really quiet."

"Then why did you leave the farm?" asked a puzzled chipmunk.

"It wasn't as we thought," explained Marcus. "It was scary. We didn't realize how good we had it living here in the forest. Now we appreciate it."

Then Marcella said, "You can sing and make all the noise you want. Now we like living in the forest."

"Caw!  Caw!  Caw!" went the happy crows as they began to sing.

"Chop!  Chop!  Chop!" went the busy beavers as they began to work.

"Chip!  Chip!  Chip!" yelled the playful chipmunks as they raced around the log.

Then Marcus turned to Marcella and said, "Even with all the noise and hard work, I'm so happy to be living in the forest. We surely were foolish for not appreciating what we had."

"I agree!" said Marcella, beaming from ear to ear. "The forest is a *wonderful* place to live."